EMERALD'S REVENGE

SIN IN THE CITY

EMERALD'S REVENGE

SIN IN THE CITY

SYDNEY RENEÉ

PREFACE

Love is beautiful. Love is sweet. Love is all we need….said
no one in this novella. Periodically, revenge is the answer.
Don't get me wrong, I love a good love story, but if you're
looking for that in this book, prepare to be freed from
illusion. Sometimes these characters need to suffer a slow,
brutal death, and I'm pleased to give it to them.

The love may have exited the room, but the twists and
turns remain.

1

DOMINIC VASQUEZ

"Soon, you won't have to worry about spending another night alone. You and my son will be my priority from here on out."

Akira, my long-time girlfriend and the mother of my six-year-old son, stood across the room from me, leaned against the dresser, and cried as she watched me pack my bags, again.

"You've been saying that bullshit for six years now. Yet, here I am again watching you pack up to go be with her."

"She's my wife, Akira. What did you expect when you signed up to be with me?"

"I don't know, but it wasn't this," she said, waving her hands around. "I'm in this big house alone with our son, and our time with you is very limited. It's not fair," she whined.

Watching her breakdown every time I had to go home to my wife was heartbreaking, but she signed up for this life the moment she decided to keep pursuing a relationship with a married man. For almost eight years, Akira stood by my side, watching me give the world to my wife, and allowing me to have a few extra women on the side. Emerald didn't play that shit. She knew of a few women I dealt with, but she was very vocal regarding her feelings. In the words of Emerald Vasquez, I had her fucked all the way up.

At the start of our affair, she wasn't supposed to be anything more than a fling, but then she ended up pregnant, and when I found out she was going to have a boy, I was ecstatic. Finally, I would have someone to pass my legacy down to, and I made sure of that with my lawyers and the executor of my will. Unlike Akira, who was dying for love and the perfect family, Emerald was against having children. I know she was young when I approached her and asked her to be my wife. Still, I thought eventually she'd be ready to settle down and solely focus on being a housewife, but she enjoyed running shit, going on vacations, and spending up all my got-damn money. A kid was just going to get in the way. Having a baby on her didn't make things any better. Most times she acted like he didn't exist. No amount of love or gifts I showered her with would manipulate her into playing stepmom to a side baby. It made my decision to divorce her effortless. I couldn't be with a woman who didn't love my child.

Walking over to Akira, I pulled her in close, looking down into big brown eyes. "I'm going to divorce her sooner than you think."

"You promise," she said, looking up at me sadly.

Taking hold of her hand, I guided her to the suitcase on the bed. On top was a manila envelope.

"Here," I said, handing the envelope to Akira.

Hesitant, she pulled the envelope to her chest and said, "Is this the real thing? You told me this same story before."

"But I've never shown you papers."

Slowly opening it, Akira pulled out the documents and scanned them. "You signed already?"

"I told you I was serious about making our family official." I gripped her waist to pull her in for a kiss. "Just give it some time, and I promise it's you and me forever."

5

2

Dominic Vasquez

FOUR MONTHS LATER...

Dominic: Don't be mad, but I won't be able to see you this weekend.

Akira: Why not? I thought we were on the same page again.

Dominic: We are. I'm taking her on a trip to break the news. It's finally happening.

Akira: I love you Dominic.

After deleting my messages, I pulled up to our home, where Emerald was waiting outside with her bags.

"Look who decided to show up." Emerald rolled her eyes as I approached her.

"I'm so sorry, Princess," I said, leaning in to kiss her, but she moved her head to the side. "Aww, are you going to do Papi like that for real? I had some last-minute business to handle at the casino before we headed out. You know Rico is forgetful."

"I guess," she said, turning back toward me and planting those big, juicy lips on mine. "Here you go," she handed me her bag. There were two extras behind it.

"Damn woman, what you got in these. We're only going to be gone for a few days," I said, loading her bags into the back of the Range.

"With us, you can never be so sure," she smiled. "It might turn into a permanent stay."

"I bet you'd like that," I said, closing the trunk, then helping her into the car.

I might have been about to end our marriage, but I would still treat Emerald with all the respect in the world. Despite all my cheating, I loved the ground that woman walked on; however, some things just aren't meant to last forever. I was just hoping she would still be willing to work with me once I served her these papers. My investors would be furious if they found out Emerald wasn't around to provide her input.

The ride to our destination was silent, turning our hour-and-a-half trip into what felt like three. Emerald didn't say much as we traveled to Pahrump, Nevada. She gazed out the window and occasionally sang along to the music playing. It wasn't until we pulled onto the property that her big green eyes lit up with excitement.

"Now this is nice," she said, opening the car door and sprinting to the entrance of the one-bedroom adobe-style home I had rented for us.

I had no business getting us a one-bedroom home, but if this would be my last time with Emerald as my wife, I would enjoy every last minute of it. One last dip in that ocean wouldn't be a sin.

"You sure it's not too quaint for your lavish taste?"

Laughing, Emerald gazed at me lovingly and said, "It's perfect."

3

Emerald Vasquez

"It's time to wake up." I smacked Dominic across the face to wake him up from his slumber.

Dazed and confused, he had no clue what was going on until he tried to move and realized he was hog-tied to a chair.

"What the fuck, Emerald" he said calmly. "How did I end up like this?"

"So about that," I grinned. "That delicious meal I made for you. I put sedatives in your mashed potatoes and crushed a few pills into your wine. Nothing that will kill you."

"Are you laughing? This isn't a joke. Untie me, Emerald."

"Do you know how hard it was to get your ass in that chair and tie you up? I don't think so." I chuckled and walked in front of him.

I couldn't believe I let that triflin' husband of mine fuck me till the sunrise, knowing he no longer wanted me to carry his last name. The way he kissed every each of my body before devouring my pussy, and then making love to me would have one thinking this marriage would last for at least twenty more years, but Dominic had that effect on women. Instead, he was attempting to replace me with someone new- a bitch who was truly unworthy of his love and his funds.

"You were supposed to be different," I yelled, pacing back and forth in front of him.

We were still in the middle of the kitchen. The house Dominic rented offered the perfect open layout. Everything resembled one large living room connected by wide entryways. Tonight was our last night here, and everything felt so perfect. Dominic had been incredibly attentive to me this weekend, and I almost felt guilty for what I was doing.

"I am, Princess," he tried to assure me, but I could tell he was nervous.

"You turned out to be exactly like the rest of these no-good-ass-men. No fucking respect for the woman who would risk it all for you. I would have died for you. Do you know that?"

Before he could answer, I kicked the chair that I tied him to and watched it break into pieces, the way our relationship had, because he couldn't keep his dick in his pants. Throughout our marriage, I'd been nothing but a loyal, devoted wife, and he chose to fool around on me with who knows how many women.

"Did you even love me? You couldn't have." The thoughts in my head were coming out fast as lightning.

I can't believe I'm about to do this. My husband was the king of my castle, and I treated him as such. Before him, I'd been in a relationship with a little boy who didn't know my value, didn't respect or love me, but only saw me as a way to get by. Dominic saw my potential and encouraged me to boss up. I should have vetted him longer before committing my life to him. A year after my last relationship ended, Dominic spotted me in the strip club, and that same day, he swore I would be his wife. I thought he was a damn fool, but a few months later, I was indeed Mrs. Vasquez.

"Why are you doing this to me, Emerald?" He groaned while trying to wiggle out of his zip ties. "This isn't you."

"You don't know who I am," I circled him, "because if you had known me, you would have known disloyalty doesn't sit well with me."

"I know you're my wife. I know I fucked up, but I love you dearly, and you love me." He tried to soften me up.

"Then why did you play me for a fool, Dominic?" I stopped in front of him and kicked him in the stomach. "Why did you waste years of my life?" I kicked him again. "Why did you tell me you loved me if you were just going to give it to someone else?" I kicked him once more.

"E-e-emerald," he struggled to breathe.

"You know I don't like to share, especially dick that's supposed to belong to me and only me," I bent down and screamed in his face.

"I'm sorry," he whimpered, but his sorry didn't mean shit to me and never would.

It's just another lie I had to hear. If he were sorry, he wouldn't have left me lonely every chance he got. He would have continued to love me the way he had initially. He would have never put me in a position to turn into this woman, a woman full of resentment. He would have said sorry before we reached this point if he were sorry.

"You're not sorry, Dominic." I knelt in front of him and took hold of his face…that got damn face handpicked by God himself. I squeezed it as hard as I could, leaving indents of my fingers on his cheeks before kissing his busted lip. I licked off the blood and stood to walk away.

"I am. I swear I am," he pleaded, tears filling his brown eyes. "I love you. We can make this work. I'll never hurt you again," he cried, but I knew it wasn't for me. He wanted to save himself and go home to his side bitch, but it was too late for that.

"I wish that were true, my love." I walked over to the table. "I really do, but your time is up."

"W-h-what are you going to do?" His thick eyebrows raised, and fear painted his face.

"I'm doing what's necessary."

"No, you're overreacting. It doesn't have to come to this. Just let me go," he begged.

"I hate that I have to do this to you." I walked back over to him and poured gasoline on him. He screamed, but no one could hear him out here. There was nothing but desert surrounding us.

"You were my favorite. We had the potential to be a wonderful couple and dominate together, and we could have continued to build our empire," I paused. "But now, everything we ever were has to go up in flames."

"Emerald, please don't do this to me…to us," he cried. "I love you. I married you. I chose you," he screamed.

Making a path to the door with gasoline, I grabbed my belongings and struck a match. I stood in the doorway, watching him cry and scream, reflecting on our good times. I should have felt sad, but I didn't. I felt nothing- nothing that would have compelled me to walk back inside to save his life. It's not like he would have saved mine. I flung the match and watched the flames rush toward him. He attempted a last-minute escape, but there was no use; he was trapped. The flames engulfed him, and he screamed out in agony.

"I hope you rot in hell," I said before walking to the car parked up the road.

4

EMERALD VASQUEZ

ONE YEAR LATER...

I sat inside the Columbarium crying as if I weren't the one who ended my husband's life. Today marked a year since his horrible death, and it was bittersweet. Today was the day I burned him to a crisp and walked away with my head held high. Some days I'm surprised I got away with it, but I'm Emerald Vasquez…*How could I not have gotten away with murder as fine and resourceful as I am?* It's beneficial to know people in high places.

Dominic's death was ruled a freak accident, and no one had any proof that I had been away with him on his solo retreat. Since I had a life insurance policy on him and the house he bought me for our wedding was in my name, I still got to live a life of luxury, but had it been up to him, I wouldn't have gotten anything. Almost everything we had, went to that bitch from Jersey he was fucking behind my back. When I found out about his side family, it was like my heart was ripped from my chest and then stomped out. It was gone, no longer beating. I was still filled with so much hate…so much rage. I'd probably never get over the pain of losing him forever.

Every time I visited his resting place, I wanted to bring him back to life just to kill him again for what he did. I thought I'd be over his betrayal by now, but I'm not. I vowed my life, love, and everything else to this man; I was merely the main attraction. I was the woman he liked to brag about, the one he showcased like a fucking showhorse. He utilized me to attract the big investors, and then he'd put me back in my stable once he got what he wanted. I sometimes resented him for it, but I miss him even as I sit here today.

In the beginning, it didn't bother me. I was young, naive, and fascinated with the dollar signs. Dominic bled green, and I was benefiting from it all. Thanks to him, I could get out of those dirty-ass strip clubs and help out at **The Vasquez Palace**. On top of that, he adored me, and damn, was he a sight to see. Always in a tailored suit, a fresh haircut that looked and shined like the sea, a smile as bright as a lone star in the pitch black, and an ass like a baseball player.

Dominic Vasquez was a big-shot casino owner from a family of lawyers and drug dealers, but they were most known for their casino empire, **The Vasquez Palace**. They had casinos in New Jersey, New York, Louisiana, and Las Vegas. Dominic inherited the billion-dollar industry when his mother and father were killed in a business deal gone wrong. He was 24 and fresh out of college with a master's in business. All his focus went into the empire; that's what I thought, but the man literally had some tricks up his sleeve. The women were fascinated by him. He was charming, intelligent, and sexy as fuck, but he was mine, and I took pride in knowing that.

"Why the fuck are you here?"

Ugh, this bitch.

15

I watched Dominic's stupid-ass baby mother approach me. That bitch knows this is my day to spend time with him. She should have waited until tomorrow to visit like a good side bitch should.

"Why the fuck do you think? Ole stupid ass."

"To keep up an appearance," she said, walking up to me. "I know what you did."

"And what is it that I did?" I asked, looking her up and down.

I could tell she'd been enjoying the benefits of Dominic's death—dressed in designer from head to toe and dripping in diamonds. You could tell she was a bitch from Jersey no matter how put-together she attempts to look. She still looked tacky as fuck, with that busted-ass red ponytail in her head. It didn't complement her beautiful cocoa skin well. Oh, and that annoying voice irked me every time. Bitch always sounded like she was sick. I don't know what Dominic saw in her. I know for a fact I looked better. I know I fucked better too.

"You took away my first love, my son's father."

"Fuck you and your son," I said with no remorse, "You both can rot in hell with him. That's the only way you'll get your fake family back."

"I can't believe he married you." She spat at my feet, and it took everything in me not to drag her across the damn ground.

"Believe it. You saw what it was. He loved me until his last dying breath." I pushed past her.

I should kill this bitch and then raise her fucking son as my own. That would be sweet, I think as I make my way to my car. I stopped in my tracks when I saw Rico Adams coming toward me. Rico was Dominic's right-hand man. If I hadn't known any better back then, I would have thought they were brothers as protective as Dominic was over him. I didn't understand Dominic's loyalty to him. Where Dominic saw family, all I saw was a fine-ass snake trying to make its way into my garden. On numerous occasions, he made it known how much he wanted to slide between my thighs. I'd flirt for enjoyment but never let it extend beyond that. Don't get me wrong, Rico is fine and, at times, intriguing. He has skin like butter, hair fine as silk, and eyes like the ocean, beautiful and profound. Oh, and the teeth. I'd say they were fake if I didn't know any better, except his bottom tooth was slightly pushed back. I had never met a man so perfect If I had seen him before Dominic or If I knew he was living this secret life, we definitely would have fucked.

"Looking like money." I do a quick scan of Rico.

"Yeah, decided to get dressed today," he said, brushing his waves.

"I see. Everyone must have been missing Dominic today. His baby mom is in there." I motioned my head toward the Columbarium in disgust.

"Well, actually," he said, putting his brush into his back pocket, "I came with her. If you get my drift?"

"So you're fucking her?" I smirked. "Sometimes you gotta go for the next best thing, but it would have been a real win if you came back for me." I kissed him on the cheek.

Akira watched us from afar, so I hugged him tightly, looking directly at her. "When you get bored with her…come and see me."

5

AKIRA SHARPE

Nothing about Emerald rubbed me the right way. I knew her ass was crazy no matter the effort she took to hide behind her innocent smile. She was wicked, an absolute bitch. Men only wanted her because of her pretty green almond eyes, fat ass, voluptuous thighs, killer waist, big tits, and long hair.

If Dominic honestly loved her, he wouldn't have kept fooling around with me, and I damn sure wouldn't be living in Vegas. All he needed was a bit of time, and we would have been living the life we dreamed of having together, but I'm positive that evil bitch cut it short. I wished he had left her when I asked him to. I was the one with his heir and his heart.

He planned on leaving her a year before he died; he even talked to a divorce lawyer, but two months later, he ripped up the papers and told me it wasn't the right time, as the two of them still had business to get done. I didn't talk to him for months, and I was so pissed I hadn't let him see our son. The constant back and forth was draining and an environment I didn't want our son to become accustomed to. Then, four months before he died, he told me he wanted to leave Emerald for good. He removed her from his will, bought us a beautiful family home in Nevada, and ensured our son Dario would inherit the family business. Since Emerald never produced a child, he was the only remaining male in the Vasquez line.

My world almost ended when I discovered he had died in a house fire while on the trip he took her on. I knew Emerald had something to do with it. The idea of him leaving her for me killed Emerald. She had the most to lose, and I had a gut feeling she figured out she wouldn't get anything except their house. Somehow, she had still found a way to live a million-dollar lifestyle.

The night before Dominic died, he texted me, saying he would take her on a weekend getaway to break the news to her gently. I relayed this information to the police, who didn't take me seriously. They regarded me as his heartbroken mistress and dismissed me by claiming no evidence pointed in her direction. I called bullshit, but no one wanted to believe me, not even Rico, and I was fucking him.

"What the fuck did she want?"

"Me," he chuckled, prompting me to storm past him, shoving him out of the way. I had noticed how he marveled at her whenever she was near.

"I'm just playing Ki," he said quickly. "She was simply saying it was nice seeing me after so long."

"I don't care for her," I said, leaning in for a kiss, aware that she would likely be watching us.

"I'm sure she feels the same." He kissed me back. "You done visiting your baby daddy?"

"I'm out here, aren't I?"

"You don't have to be a smart ass because you have beef with Emerald." He shook his head.

"I couldn't care less about her," I snap, knowing how much I hate her.

"Let's get to this meeting. The only way I'll be able to take over the downtown casino is if you sign your shares over to me."

"Is that all you care about right now?" I rolled my eyes and headed to the car.

Pulling my arm, he stopped me and said, "I'm handling all this shit anyways. I have been since that nigga died. Handing over one casino is not going to harm anybody. It's not like you enjoy being involved. You want to sit pretty and spend money."

Glaring at his hand wrapped around my arm, I snatched away from him. "Just because you're fucking me doesn't mean you running shit."

"Don't act like you don't like that shit. If you didn't, you wouldn't have let me bust that pussy wide open whenever that nigga was too busy spending time with his wife. For all you know, that baby ain't even his," he said and walked to the car.

"You're an asshole, Rico."

"But you're still here, aren't you? Bring yo ass on," he said, getting in the car.

6

Emerald Vasquez

Sitting in my car, I laughed hysterically as I watched jealousy overtake Akira. That bitch couldn't stand that the men in her life would jump off a fucking bridge to be with me. I was married to Dominic, and she acted like she was the one who lost a fucking husband, and Rico…well, he's just something good to look at, but I could take it a step further if I wanted. He'd be an easy one to hook.

Akira should have kept her ass in New Jersey. I thought she would have left Vegas after I got rid of Dominic; there was nothing here for her. She could have looked over his casinos in Jersey and New York if that's what she wanted, but seeing as she's fucking Rico, I would have stayed too. I can tell he's about to take advantage of her already. I could warn her about his snake ass, but fuck that; she deserves whatever she has coming.

Pulling out of the cemetery, I headed to my beautiful home in the southern highlands. With the money from Dominic's policy and the sale of the house we shared, I moved into a million-dollar home in one of the best neighborhoods in Las Vegas. I was also able to open up the dance studio I'd been dreaming of for almost a decade. All the hottest dancers in the industry come to see me, and the strippers that want to make a name for themselves shell out all their income to secure a spot on my calendar. My motto has always been, "You need to spend money to make money." These girls would make triple by learning the tricks I had up my retired g-strings.

As the front of my house came into view, I spotted Detective Brown on my porch. Either he had terrible news for me, or he was itching for some pussy, which I'd happily give to him most days, but after seeing Akira, I wasn't in the mood to offer up any ass, no matter how good he put the dick on me with his fine chocolate self.

Brown was one of the most handsome men I'd ever come across, and the dick in his pants was made of magic, hitting every spot that was known to drive a bitch insane. But what I valued most was how he kept the authorities from sniffing around me or anyone associated with me. I was off limits, and everyone knew it. I wasn't a fan of the police, but having Detective Brown on my team was the smartest thing for me. I wouldn't be able to get away with half the shit I did if it weren't for him. That doesn't mean it didn't take this killer pussy and some heavy blackmail to get him to stay in line. Brown was a man who didn't take kindly to being told what to do, but if I ever went down for my dirt, I was making sure he was going down beside me, and I reminded him of that every time he came around trippin'.

Getting out of the car, I walked over to Brown with a massive smile. "Hey, handsome. What brings you to my doorstep?"

"Can a man pop up just because?" He asked, leaning against my door and rubbing his beard.

"I'm not a fan of pop-ups, no matter how sexy the man doing them is," I smirked, "and when you do pop up, I know it's nothing good coming out of your beautiful mouth."

"Let me in, and you'll find out," he smirked.

Kicking off my shoes and walking toward my kitchen, I grabbed a beer for him and a green juice for myself. "So, Wassup?" I asked, leaning over the counter.

"Your husband—"

"Dead-husband," I interrupt.

"Your *husband's* baby's mother is trying to get the case reopened."

"That bitch will find herself in an urn right next to him if she doesn't stop fucking with me." I rolled my eyes to the back of my head. "What the fuck is she saying now?"

Chuckling, he said, "She came into the station yelling at the top of her lungs that we didn't do our job right and that his death should have been ruled a homicide. Luckily, I was there when it happened."

"Why is that?"

"She had text messages and a photo that proved you were with him that night." He raised an eyebrow.

I almost lost my footing. This wasn't the news I was expecting to hear at all. I couldn't believe this bastard still managed to fuck me over before he died. I wanted to find her and slit her fucking throat; unfortunately, I'd be the first on the suspect list.

"Well…?"

"I took her phone. I told her it was evidence and that I needed it. It's destroyed. Before you ask, I checked with the phone company, and there's no exchange record. The phone she had was a burner they used in case Dominic got into trouble…I'm assuming."

"But Detective," I paused, "what if she backed everything up?"

"Then you're fucked, pretty eyes."

"What the fuck do I have you for then?"

"Relax," he said, reaching over to rub my face. "I'll see what else I can do."

I loved how his semi-rough hands felt against my skin and how he'd do whatever to protect me.

"Thank you, Detective," I turned and kissed the hand on my face.

"You know I love it when you call me *Detective*."

"Then come over here and show me, *Detective*."

I said I wasn't in the mood to give up any ass, but the man was hard to resist. His devilish grin and midnight eyes forever pulled me in. Part of me was terrified of this man, but the other was mesmerized. I tried my hardest to act like he was a fun fuck that I could get rid of at any time, but no matter what, my body gravitated his way.

"Happily," he said, strolling to my side of the kitchen and hiking me up on the counter.

Pulling his hoodie over his head, I admired his smooth mahogany skin and explored his defined abs with my hands. The man knew he would be deep inside me before our visit ended, the way he was oiled up and scented down.

"Tell me what you want." He gripped my neck with just the right amount of pressure and glided his tongue across my lips.

"I want you, *Detective*."

"Tell me exactly what you want." He squeezed tighter.

"I want you to fuck me."

Yanking down his sweatpants, his dick sprang forward, and my pussy throbbed at the sight. No matter how many times I've held it in my hand, put it in my mouth, or guided it into my pussy, I was amazed at the length and width. Every time we fucked, it was like my cherry being popped again.

Putting his hands up my skirt, he moved my thong to the side and dipped his finger inside me.

"Already wet," he said, giving me that devilish smile I loved.

"For you...*Always*," I moaned as he stroked my insides.

Replacing his fingers with his dick, he pushed into me, stretching me out until I was filled. Speeding up his pace, my body quaked, and I matched his tempo as I fucked him back. Planting my hands on his firm ass, I pushed him deeper.

"I love that dick, *Detective*."

"Tell me again," he groaned as his tempo sped and he pressed down on my clit.

"*Detective*," I whimpered, "I love your dick so fucking bad," I said as an orgasm took control of my body, causing me to wrap my arms tightly around his neck.

"Damn, you look good as fuck when you come," he said, sweat dripping from his head.

"Cum for me, *Detective*," I demanded, squirting all over his dick and stomach.

Wrapping his arm around my waist, his shoulders tightened, and he slammed one hand down on the counter and pounded as deep into my pussy as he could.

"Fuuuuck," he grunted as I came again, "I'm about to bust."

7

RICO ADAMS

"I can't believe you agreed to let her run the gentleman's club. It's bad enough I have to potentially see her every time I visit Dom, but now I have to see her at the casino's gentleman's club?"

"Baby, you don't even be in there like that."

"That's beside the fucking point. I don't want her running that spot."

"How else would we get those investors to agree to the deal? I know you don't like her, but she's the reason we have all this shit, and to keep the money flowing, we need her," I said, trying to get Akira to understand Emerald was the only way for us to get the club open.

"Not using her name," Akira picked up a vase and threw it near my head. "That bitch killed Dominic, and now you're going to have her all up in his Casino running a damn strip club."

"My casino." I corrected her. "That's my shit, and I'll have whoever the fuck I want working in that bitch. Got it?"

"You know what? It don't even matter because soon that bitch is going to be rotting in jail, and I can move on with my life."

"Is this not moving on?" I said, turning in a circle. "You living in this fat ass crib, got designer on your body, all the cars you want, but don't drive, and you're getting fucked exactly how you like."

"That's not what I mean. I want her gone," she whined.

Akira was pissing me off when it came to her beef with Emerald. She was living the life she had begged Dominic for. I don't know why she couldn't let this theory about Emerald killing him go. Even if she had, the nigga deserved it. He thought he was so much better than everyone, and he didn't truly love Emerald or Akira, for that matter. He liked how they looked beside him and how Emerald elevated his businesses. Emerald needed a nigga like me. Not only would I have taken care of her, but I would have treated her like the Goddess she was. Instead, I got stuck with Akira's ass. Don't get me wrong, she's an incredible chick to kill time with, talk to, cuddle a little and fuck, but she complains constantly. Daily that woman gives me a headache and over the tiniest shit.

"You need to let that shit go. He's gone, and I'm here. I've been here this entire time taking care of you, loving on you when he wouldn't. I don't know why you tried acting like you were in love with that nigga."

"I was, Rico."

"Save that shit for somebody who'll believe you. You only wanted Emerald's life, and now you've got it. Go back to that damn station and tell whoever you talked to you take back what you said."

"Or what?"

"Or you can go meet that nigga in hell," I wrapped my hands tight around her throat, "since you want to be with him so got damn bad."

Akira loved testing me. I swear she got a kick out of me roughing her up. Every time I touched this bitch she fell deeper in love. I wasn't even that kind of nigga. I never put my hands on a woman until I met her ass. It started on some kinky type shit. She wanted a nigga to hit her. I was skeptical at first. I wasn't trying to end up in jail because of some woman's kink fetish, but when I gave in, her pussy turned into a damn ocean, and I loved how that shit felt on my dick. Eventually, shit took a turn. Her stank-ass attitude and constant obsession with Dominic and his wife enraged me, and those hits weren't for her pleasure but more to relieve my frustration.

"Calm down, Ri," she said, clawing at my hands.

"This what you wanted, right? This that shit you like, right?" I tightened my grip as she tried to speak.

"I-I-I'll let it go," she finally said.

"I'm serious, Ki. I can't have you fucking up the business over a dead nigga." I eased up my grip so she could speak clearly.

"I hear you. Now let me go before Dario gets here and sees you acting a damn fool."

"And stop acting like that little nigga is Dominic's son. You're pissing me off with that shit."

"He is," she lied through those false ass teeth of hers.

That little nigga looked nothing like Dominic but a smaller version of me. Bitch tried to say he looked like her uncle on her daddy's side. I'll know for sure in a few weeks when the DNA results come back. I swabbed his ass when she wasn't home. There was no way I would let my son keep calling another man daddy, a dead one at that.

29

"Yeah, keep lying to yourself. You know I was bussin'
nuts in you left and right."

"Want to bust one now," she said, yanking my belt.

"Nah, I'm good. You fucked up my mood."

8

Emerald Vasquez

TWO WEEKS LATER...

"Great class, ladies." I clapped and wiped myself down with a towel.

I was whooped, and the day wasn't nearly over yet, but it was worth it. I loved doing my job. Some days I was tired, but the training kept me in shape, flexible in bed, and all my bills paid. There were at least 15 people in total who came into class for today's morning session. That was a quick $2000 for an hour. I still had an afternoon and evening class and a private lesson, which I charged double for. I could make $8,000 to $10,000 easily on a daily basis.

"I'll be back for your second class later today," my girl Phoenix said before packing her belongings.

"Are you working the pole tonight?"

"Hell no. A bitch would fall and break her neck after the tricks you had us working on today. That shit is not for the weak. I'm going home, soaking, replenishing myself, and then be back here tonight," she said.

"And you ain't told not one lie. Y'all want to make extra money, not end up on disability," I laughed, spinning the towel around my head.

"You too fine for that ass to be stuck in the house, cripple." Rico was standing at the class entrance, leaning against the door in an emerald green slim-fit suit, with a white button-up that I'm positive he purposely left undone to show off his gold chain, pecs, and chiseled abs. I took in the view.

"Who is that?" Phoenix asked, practically drooling.

"Girl, get yo ass out of here. I'll see you tonight." I laughed and showed her off. Rico managed to eye fuck her the whole way out like the creep he was. He could be with any woman he wanted, so I wasn't sure why he settled with Akira instead of living like a bachelor.

"See you later, sexy," Rico said.

"No, he won't," I yelled. "Get yo ass over her and stop flirting with my girl before I tell your ugly ass girlfriend."

"Why you gotta be so damn rude?" He caressed his face and walked my way.

Whenever he moved, it looked like he was gliding across the floor, and I couldn't help but get turned on a little. He was still fine, no matter how much of a jerk he was.

"So, what brings you here?" I asked, picking up a fresh towel and taking my bottle of alcohol to disinfect the poles for my next class.

"Is there somewhere I can sit?"

"You see me cleaning. What do you want?"

"Damn, Emerald. You might be pretty, but you mean as hell."

"Not mean enough since you're here in my face." I put my hands on my hips and waited for him to speak.

Rico went ghost as soon as we had a funeral for Dominic. I hadn't expected him to check in, but I didn't need him acting like we were best friends. I can give a damn about how fine the man is.

"I have a business proposition for you, and I'm praying you say yes."

"Keep talking."

"I've taken ownership of Dominic's casino, and we are opening a gentleman's club. Please run it. You'll have complete control. You can hire your staff, girls, and DJ, and I'll cover all expenses. I need you to bring in the crowd."

"Benefits? A retirement plan? Paid time off?"

"You'll have all that and more, Emerald. I need you to say yes."

"How long do I have to decide?"

"End of the day tomorrow," he whispered because he knew that shit was crazy. *How do you ask someone to manage a business at the last minute?*

"Nigga. You are so unprofessional." I shook my head and rolled my eyes. "I'll think about it and let you know. I doubt your bitch is on board with this."

"Trust me; she won't be a problem. I can guarantee that."

"And if she becomes one?"

"Then I'll handle it," he said, stepping behind me. We were close, and I could feel his print hardening against my ass. *I think he might be working with something nice*, I think, then pull myself out of the gutter.

"Back up. You're nowhere near ready for me." I winked at him. "I'll call you tonight or tomorrow with my answer."

Pulling me into a hug, he kissed the top of my head and said, "I'm counting on it," then exited the room.

. . . .

My private lesson with Phoenix ended around 10:00 PM. The ride to my house didn't take but 15 minutes max, and I managed to make it there in ten. Despite the time, it was still slightly warm out, with a cool breeze. We were experiencing a clear night sky; all that gleamed were the stars and the moon.

I was done for once my lesson ended. My arms and legs were turning to jello. I could have lain on the floor and called it a night, but I needed a shot of tequila and a bath full of Epsom salt. A massage would have been the icing on the cake, but I guess I'd have to wait another day. Slipping off my clothes, I took a quick shower, dried off, and walked my bare ass downstairs to make a drink. The combination of tequila, cranberry, lime juice, and a splash of Grand Marnier made for the perfect drink to sit in my hot tub and unwind. Turning on my Bluetooth, I put on some Sade and stepped into the Jacuzzi—sinking into the hot water, I rested against the headrest and closed my eyes.

In times like these, I missed Dominic before realizing he was a cheat. The man I met all those years ago dedicated his days to making me happy. I remember listening to music and talking for hours while he massaged my feet. We'd make love for hours and shower together before falling asleep wrapped in each other. I had a partner, a companion I could come to at the end of the night to vent my frustration and share my ideas of becoming a famous choreographer.

Meanwhile, I wasn't the only woman he'd been sharing his life and dreams with. There were multiple, but Akira bothered me the most. I despised her. I hated everything about her. Because of her, I had to dispose of the man I wanted to spend the rest of my life with. Had I known our relationship would go up in flames due to his sins, I would have never said yes to his proposal. I could have sucked it up and let him keep sleeping around, but those two were in too deep. I knew he only planned a trip because he wanted to give her everything that was *mine*, including the ring. I found a copy of the divorce papers two weeks before we were supposed to leave. I ignored them, thinking he'd change his mind. That was until I checked his call logs and saw he and Akira had been communicating every second of every hour. Every day after that, I saw nothing but red. Everything that surrounded us was hot to the touch. My love for him had been engulfed in flames and couldn't be revived.

Emerald: I'm in.

Rico: I knew you couldn't pass on an opportunity this big.

An opportunity to make Akira's life a living hell? I sure couldn't; I thought as I set my phone down and finished my drink.

AKIRA SHARPE

"You're out of your mind," I screamed at Rico. I couldn't believe he went behind my back like that. "How dare you violate my son and his privacy?" I asked, ripping up the paternity test he held to my face.

"I'm out of my mind? You're a different kind of bitch, you know that? Straight up foul as fuck," he replied in disgust. "Every day since I've become a constant in his life, I knew, and you just kept lying to my face." He stormed out of the living room and up the steps.

I knew that Rico was Dario's biological father, but Dominic cared for us. The last name Vasquez set my son up for life, and he never has to worry about where his next meal will come from or about the water being cut off when least expected. It was silly of me to believe Rico would take my word and set aside his suspicions. They shared the same eyes, had the same walk, and bore the exact same birthmark on the back of their necks. Anyone with eyes could see that they were one and the same.

"I told you I'd find out sooner than later if his little ass belonged to me. Did you assume I supported him because he was your kid?" He asked but refused to let me speak before continuing. "Negative…He reminds me too much of myself. For fucks sake, Akira, he looks like me but a shade darker.

I'm surprised Dominic didn't challenge his paternity, but I guess that pussy had him convinced he was the daddy."

"What does it matter? You're here. You didn't have to swab my son without talking to me first."

"Are you stupid? I've come to you multiple times, Akira." He clenched his fist. "You've been lying to my face for years. Those are years *I* missed out on forming a bond with my son. Years I can't reach back for. You saw dollar signs when you saw Dominic and said fuck me and my chance to be a father. It's bitches like you that make it hard to trust a bitch."

Rico paced back and forth in our bedroom. The veins in his arm were more visible than usual. Nothing I said would quiet the rage within, and admitting I saw Dominic as a meal ticket wouldn't help our situation. It was true; I deprived him of a relationship with our son because of my fucked up psyche. I never thought about what I was taking away from him, but what my son and I would gain…a whole hell of a lot.

Rico's a wonderful man; I'm sure he'd be a better husband, but that wasn't the plan. When I met Rico, he charmed me right out of my pants and catered to my every need. When Dominic disclosed that he had married the stripper he met, Rico let me cry in his arms all night. Whenever I was miserable, he was there to console me—one of those nights led to us creating a child. Despite how amazing he was to me, Dominic was the one I yearned for.

"We can fix this. We can change his last name, sit him down, and tell him you're his real father."

"The papers are already signed. We need to turn them in." He stopped pacing and grimaced at me. "As far as telling him who I am, we'll have to ease into that."

The anger smeared on his face had transformed into something I had witnessed before. I hurt him. He had a right to his feelings, but something told me he loved me and didn't know how to give all himself to me. He'd been sharing his son and me for longer than he should have, and there was no way he'd ever fully trust me or anything I had to say.

Slowly approaching him, I rested my hand on his face. The word, *sorry,* wouldn't get through to him as my touch would. There was magic in the way I caressed his beautiful face. They were medicated; an automatic relaxer.

"I was wrong," I admitted. "I'll never wrong you again."

Rico stayed silent. What I was saying wasn't getting through, and his silence was how he would discipline me.

Leaving him where he stood, I walked across the room toward the dresser that housed all my sex toys. Taking out the handcuffs and whip, I walked over to him and tucked the handle into the palm of his hand. Maintaining his position, I tore the shirt from his chest and lowered his basketball shorts and briefs. The face looking down at me may have been covered in disappointment and rage, but his dick was standing at attention, ready to destroy me. Now that I had Rico bearing his all, it was time for my punishment to begin.

Removing my clothing, I made my way to the bed, handcuffed myself to the bedpost, and waited to feel the heat from the leather whip sting my skin. The anticipation excited me in ways no one understood but Rico. I craved pain before pleasure. I could lose all control. I could scream, cry, and beg for more as loud as I wanted, well, until it was time to pick our son up from school.

"Again, Daddy," I shouted as the leather fringes smacked my ass. "Give me a beating for every year I told lies." Six, to be exact.

Rico hit me harder and harder each time, causing my pussy to pulsate. Climax was approaching, but he suddenly stopped. My body moved from side to side as my orgasm subsided.

"Why are you stopping? Punish me…punish me hard," I pleaded, but he said nothing and did nothing.

Turning my head, I saw Rico sliding a condom on. I knew he was upset. We never used condoms, but now he was treating me like a stranger. Walking toward me, with all his strength, he lifted me by the legs, positioning me horizontally, forcing me to hang on to the bedpost. He jabbed himself into my opening hard and fast, beating at my insides with the force of a million men. It hurt, but it was the kind of hurt that made me orgasm repeatedly with every stroke. His grip tightened on my thighs, and he let out a roar as I felt his dick pulsate. Pulling out of me, he walked to the bathroom without saying a word.

The sex was quick, but I got my fix from the punishment. I didn't expect him to make love to me. I wanted him to take his anger out on me. That's how I got the release I craved. Whether he hated me or not didn't matter. I loved his control, anger, and pain; we had just committed a sin, but he was the only one willing to sin with me.

10

Emerald Vasquez

"I've got some promising information," Detective Brown said on the other end of my phone.

"Shouldn't you be telling me this information in person?" I didn't trust communicating anything over the phone, especially to a police ass nigga.

"Open the door."

After hanging up the phone, I hurried to the door, ensuring to peek through the peephole before opening it. *I'm making all this money and have yet to get a door camera. That's going on my list of items to purchase as soon as possible.*

"Stop showing up at my muthafucking house unannounced." I snatched him inside. "Got me out here looking like an informant."

"Stop being dramatic. You and I are the only ones in this neighborhood that know I'm the law, and it's not like I show up here in my uniform, badge on hip, and my sirens ringing. They probably think I'm your little boyfriend," he said, smacking my ass.

"I'm sure you'd love to be, but that's beside the point." I strutted to the kitchen to finish what I had started. I was in the mood for some Cajun pasta, so I chopped up some vegetables and links before he called me.

"Well, excuse me, Mrs. Vasquez. I promise to make sure you're home, and I have permission to slide through."

"That's all I ask of you." I blew him a kiss. "So what's this *promising information* you have for me?"

"You gonna give me some of that food you're making if I divulge?" Brown asked, licking his lips. "A nigga hungry."

"If you want to spend time with me, just say that." I grinned. The detective had been showing up at my place way more than he used to. "But yeah, you can keep me company for the night. I've needed it."

Most of the time, I'd fuck the detective and send him on his way. I didn't want him to get too comfortable with our arrangement, but tonight I was willing to break my rule because my loneliness was getting the best of me. Brown knew all my dirt, so leaning on him for comfort wouldn't hurt. He was just as fucked up as I was, and unlike the other men in his department, he was more than single. No woman or kids were waiting for him back home. It's probably why he popped up at my house so much. He was just as lonely as I was.

"I want to spend time with you, Emerald. Are you going to allow me?"

"I guess you might as well get relaxed. You can tell me what I need to know when we sit down for dinner."

Brown watched my ass move around the kitchen, pulling out pots and pans, washing dishes between sauteing veggies, and whipping up my special Cajun Alfredo sauce. Not once did his eyes shift from me. They observed my every move, making me nervous. Our meeting was starting to feel like a first date.

. . . .

"Smells good," he said when I walked to the table with our plates. We had a Cajun pasta with shrimp, links, chicken, a side salad, and garlic bread. I wasn't a cook, but I could throw down when needed.

"It tastes better. I hope you favor spice because I'm a little heavy on the hand."

"You ain't tell one lie," he said after taking his first bite. His eyes watered, and I could tell he wanted to cough but was holding back.

"Damn, girl. It's mouthwatering, but I'm going to need a few Tums after this meal." He held his chest and laughed.

"I told you I'm heavy on the hand."

Once we finished eating and Brown helped me clean up the kitchen, we headed to the couch to talk business. My mind hadn't forgotten why he had shown up at my door. The last time he was here, he told me Akira wanted to put me away for the murder of Dominic, so I knew anything he needed to say to me involved her.

"I'm ready for the news," I said, plopping down next to Brown, who was sipping on nasty ass whiskey. I hated it but kept a bottle in the house for him. I got sick of him requesting it when he popped by.

"Your girl Akira came in randomly and took back her claims."

"Thank God."

"But the case was still reopened. Don't panic though. You should be good."

He must have caught a glimpse of the concern on my face because he took hold of my hand and squeezed it tight. I might have been crazy, but there was no way my pretty ass would survive in prison. If what I did that night fell back on me, we were both in for a rude awakening.

"Oh, and get this," he smirked, "when I did some digging, I found out that son of hers isn't Dominic's, but his business partners'."

I let out the most gut-wrenching laugh. I should have known she was a skimming-ass bitch. Of course, she was getting dick on the side. Dominic couldn't be with her every minute of the hour. He had a wife to cater to. One thing Dominic did was make sure he kept me satisfied. I couldn't blame her for hopping on the next best dick during her downtime.

"Does Rico know?"

"My sources tell me he's the one who went and got the test done."

Another laugh escaped me until I realized Dominic gave Akira and that little bastard *everything*. Had he known the child wasn't his, he'd be alive, and we'd still be married. I wouldn't be watching my back because I would have never lit his ass on fucking fire. She turned me into a got-damn murderer *again*. Dominic wasn't the first person I'd had to kill, but I was hoping he'd be the last. Akira was testing me, and I didn't mind adding her to my list.

"Am I able to contest Dominic's will? Do you know stuff like that?"

"Yeah, my dad was a lawyer. From what I know, you only have three months to contest a will, and seeing as you told me Dominic wrote you out of it despite you still being married at the time of his death, you wouldn't have been able to fight it."

43

"That's some bullshit." Tears started falling from my face. I was so resentful. She and her son had it *all*, and they aren't deserving. Eventually, Dominic won't mean anything to Dario because suddenly, he has a father, a father who's alive and well. At the end, Rico also lucked up on a bag. Now that he has proof Dario is his, he can ultimately take over Vasquez's billion-dollar empire. *Why did I agree to run his damn club?*

"Don't cry, Pretty Eyes." Brown placed both hands on my round face.

"You don't understand how infuriated I am."

"Let me fix that for you," he said, drying the tears and kissing each cheek. "Can I do that for you?" He continued, kissing my neck as I inhaled and exhaled slowly. I was already undone, and his hands had yet to touch me below the waist.

"Detective." I let out a low moan. The lips on that man were soft like snow, and with every light peck, my body quivered.

"Say it again," he demanded, using one hand to unbutton my blouse.

"Detective," I said softly, "fix me."

Reaching behind me, he unsnapped my Savage Fenty bra and slid it off, leaving my 38DDD breasts exposed. Bringing them into his mouth, another moan escaped my lips, as I breathed heavily. Each time he flicked his tongue on my erect nipples, my pussy cried out. She was dying of excitement. She needed to be penetrated slowly, deeply. She needed to feel every vein in his dick, and the curve in it needed to wave hello to her g-spot.

Unbuttoning my jeans, I struggled to wiggle out of them as Brown made a path with his tongue down my stomach. He wasn't one to take his time when taking me, and the foreplay had always been minimal. We were the get-in and get-out type of fuck buddies, but here on this couch, he was making love to my body.

"Let me assist you with those," he said, pushing me back on the couch.

Removing my jeans and thong in one go, he threw them to the side and palmed my entire pussy. I know he had to feel it throbbing between his hands because I felt it throughout my body. The feeling was intense, and as he massaged my pussy with the palm of his hand, looking at me intensely, I erupted. Suddenly my body was on fire, and he would be the one to put it out.

Sinking further into the couch, my back arched, Brown pulled me into him. Flinging my leg over the back, he positioning the other over his shoulder and then dived his tongue in and out my pussy, licking my slit and sucking on my clit before diving back inside. He was devouring the hell out of me. I wasn't sure I'd be able to survive this type of pussy eating. I tried to push his head back, but he held on for dear life. He was determined to make me come until I physically couldn't take anymore.

I did as I was told. I lay back and tried to relax, but the sensation was too much. His tongue slid from my pussy and into my ass. The feeling was sensational, and my body convulsed as he played with my pussy.

"D-d-detective," I stuttered as I came. My juices dripped down toward my ass, and I let out the loudest moan as he licked up my arousal. I covered my face in shame. I'd never let him see me this weak in the knees, but his mouth felt so good on me.

"Don't hide that pretty face from me," he said, pulling me onto his lap. I could feel the pre-cum on the tip of his dick. "I love that look on your face when you cum for me."

"Make me do it again," I begged, licking the rest of me off his lips.

"My pleasure."

11

EMERALD VASQUEZ

EIGHT YEARS AGO

I sat at the vanity in our all-white bedroom, putting on my makeup and hoping it would last till the end of my shift. Once again, I had an earlier-than-normal shift at *Tastee's* because the new girl had started her period and was complaining about having to work the pole. She was acting as if she were the only woman in the strip club who ever experienced a period while shaking ass. That never stopped any of the other bitches at the club from putting in a menstrual cup and getting to the bag.

As much as I wanted to say something about the inconvenience, I had money to make and a whole lot of bills to pay since my good-for-nothing boyfriend wasn't much help around the house. I did everything—cooked, cleaned, and paid all the bills. Half the time I couldn't even get this nigga to take out the trash. Every day I came closer to leaving him, but I couldn't. I had a soft spot for Taj. He was all I knew.

Applying my chocolate-colored lipliner, I watched Taj in the reflection of my mirror as he snored like a damn grizzly bear. I still didn't understand how we'd been living in Nevada for two years, and he hadn't managed to keep a steady job, yet managed to find a new bitch to cheat on me with every chance he got. As I thought about how dumb I became over this man, I noticed his phone lighting up on the nightstand non-stop. Of course he had that shit on silent.

Getting out of my chair, I tiptoed toward the edge of the bed and swiped the phone. Taj was never smart enough when it came to cheating. I didn't even have to unlock it to see the bitch I had beat up about a month ago with her legs spread wide for all the world to see, with a text that read, "I can't wait to feel you." I clearly didn't beat that bitches head in enough for her to still be throwing pussy his way. Setting the phone back on the counter, I just shook my head. I didn't have the energy to fight with this man today. I was over it, and after tonight's shift, he would know it too. It was time for him to get the fuck up out my house, since he couldn't respect me.

Numerous men were lining up to make me their woman. *Tastee's* wasn't the classiest gentlemen's club, but the money flowing through there was substantial. From CEOs to doctors to top athletes, I could be living lavishly in just a matter of days. Yet, I remained faithful to a fucking bum.

"Why you in my shit?" Taj wrapped his arm around my wrist.

Snatching away, I rolled my eyes. "First of all, no one was in your shit. I was getting ready to leave and thought it was my phone."

"Oh, my bad baby," he said, lifting up and quickly grabbing his phone, tucking it underneath him, unaware of what I had already seen. "Where you going?"

"One of us has to work, Taj."

"Ain't it kind of early to be shaking your ass for a bunch of thirsty ass niggas?" He questioned.

"If I'm not mistaken, the reason I'm shaking my ass in a dirty-ass strip club is because it was your idea. You not too bothered by it since you haven't stepped up to be the man of the house, so I can stop shaking my ass all hours of the day," I snapped and tried to grab my belongings before this conversation turned into a full blown argument. I could finish getting myself together at work.

"Emerald," Taj jumped out of bed, wrapping his lanky arms around me to pull me close. "I'm sorry," he said, leaning down and planting a kiss on the side of my neck before sucking it gently.

I used to melt from the feel of his tongue on my body. Those big, juicy lips devouring every part of me as I tugged on his curly afro. Now I slightly cringed whenever our bodies interacted.

"You're always sorry," I said, pushing him away. "For once, I wish your actions lined up with your words. I'm tired."

••••

Tonight turned out better than I thought it would be, that was until I spotted the bitch that had sent Taj a nude this morning outside of the club. She had some fucking balls showing up at my place of employment like shit was good. She had another thing coming.

Walking up to her, I didn't hesitate to wrap my fingers around every inch of hair she possessed.

49

"Didn't I tell you to stay away from my fucking boyfriend?" I punched her in the mouth. "Did I not beat the black off you enough last time?" I hit her again before she answered. "I'm so fucking sick of you bitches," I cried out, but before I could land another hit I was being pulled away from her, hair still attached to my hands.

"I want to press charges," she cried.

"I wish you would," I leaped towards her again, but was pulled back.

"Candice, you might want to take your fast ass home before I let her loose on your ass," I heard Stefan say.

He was one of my regulars and always seemed to be there to get me out of trouble before I took things too far. I enjoyed having him around, unlike the other men at the club. He was one of the only men who knew not to cross the boundaries I had set. He'd come to watch me perform and ensure I made it safely to my car afterward. I hadn't even noticed him as I left, but I guess I was too busy focused on that homewrecker. Either way, Stefan was one of the good ones, and I appreciated him. Some nights we would talk for hours, just because.

"Emerald, why is your fine ass out here acting like a wild animal? You are way too pretty to let that fast ass broad get you out of character, especially in front of the place that pays your bills."

"She deserved it," I said, tossing her hair.

Laughing, Stefan glanced at the hair on the ground and then back at me, "And what caused that kind of ass-whooping?"

"Taj got her that second ass-whooping. He is turning into a fucking nightmare," I cried to Stefan.

"What did he do this time?"

"Besides the constant cheating and disrespect…he refuses to make a name for himself. He acts like he was put on God's green earth for my ass to care for him. I'm so tired of coming home to a dirty-ass house and being scolded for working a job he forced me into."

"Em, I've been told you that little nigga don't deserve a woman like you. I don't know why you stay," Stefan said, pulling me into a hug.

"I need to get away from him before I'm stuck living like this." I cried. "I'm thinking about putting him out."

"I can help you with whatever you need, but you have to be serious about leaving him this time."

I'd been in a tainted-ass relationship with Taj for far too long, and I was only keeping on because I loved him. I cherished the ground he walked on. I was convinced he could do no wrong. When my friends said he was no good, I let their concerns go in one ear and out the other. Taj is the whole reason my ass is in here mounting poles and doing backflips like a damn acrobat. I could have been making my dreams as a choreographer come true. I didn't spend years in performing arts programs and taking dance classes all hours of the day to be shaking my ass in dirty-ass **Tastee's** strip joint.

"I'm serious, but the only way I'm going to be able to get away from him is to do the unthinkable," I whispered. "He's never going to let me just walk away from him…from *us.*"

"Baby girl, I can't let you get your hands dirty. You have too much going for you."

"Then what am I supposed to do, Stefan?"

"That's for me to figure out. Go home and pack a bag. I have a little studio on the other side of town. You can stay there while we figure this out, free of charge."

"I shouldn't have to leave the house I'm paying for, Stefan."

"I'm not saying you have to leave for good, but at least until you calm down and we figure out how to get that nigga out your house without causing a scene."

"You're truly a lifesaver," I said, throwing my arms around him.

"Only when it comes to you." He smiled and kissed me on the cheek. "Text me when you're packed up and ready to head my way."

••••

"Let me go, you crazy bitch."

I had a fist full of hair in my hand for the second time tonight, and this time I saw nothing but red. I couldn't believe what I had walked into. Taj tried his hardest to loosen my grip, but my adrenaline was pumping like crazy. I could have sent the bitch through the wall, as mad as I was.

"I do everything for you. *Everything*," I yelled as I dragged the woman from the bedroom to the front door, kicking and screaming, "and you do me like this."

"Baby," he said, jumping out of the bed and following behind us.

"Open the fucking door," I shouted at Taj.

"Chill."

"I said open the *fucking* door."

"Baby, let her go. The bitch is gonna be bald if you hold on any tighter."

"You're worried about this white bitch's hair when I just caught her riding the fuck out of your bare-ass dick, you dirty bastard. You should be worried about me leaving your stupid ass and possibly catching an STD."

I turned around and punched him in the face. My wrath was no longer directed toward her. He had me fucked up for the last time. I knew I should have left this sham of a relationship years ago.

"My *fine-thick-ass* pays the fucking bills in this house, and you want to fuck on ugly ass bitches in it." I punched him again, and this time he reacted and backhanded me, causing me to fall back on the floor. The woman he was fucking took her opportunity and ran out of the house naked.

"Calm down, baby. You're overreacting, and it's not like this is the first bitch you caught me cheating on you with."

He was right. I let him skate over and over again. I figured if he was coming home to me, it was alright if he fooled around with other females here and there, but *never* in his life had he brought them into *our* home, got them into *our* bed, and fucked them on *my* silk sheets.

"Fuck you," I yelled. "I hate you and what you've made of me."

The whole room went red as anger took over. I loved Taj with everything in me, but all he fucking did was use me and disrespect me. Now he was putting his hands on me over a bitch.

"Emerald, I'm sorry. Let's talk, baby. Please."

I heard nothing he said as I walked towards the kitchen, opened the drawer next to the stove, and found the biggest knife I could find. I must have blacked out soon as I slammed the drawer shut because I don't know how I ended up like this. I was sitting on top of him, coated in blood, grasping a butcher knife while a pool of blood formed underneath us.

I absolutely overreacted, I thought as I dropped the knife, but I wasn't sorry. I bent forward and kissed his lips repeatedly before whispering, "Rot in hell," in his ear.

Rushing to the kitchen sink, I washed off my hands before heading to my bag for my phone.

"Stefan…I did a terrible thing."

"Send me your address. I'm on the way."

12

RICO ADAMS

[Present] Six Months Later...

Walking into **EMERALDZ,** I knew I had made the right choice. Emerald was built to run a place like this. I saw why Dominic refused to let her go. She could make a fortune effortlessly. How she ended up in a strip club dancing for dollars every night? I never questioned. All I knew was that Dominic was mesmerized. When he wasn't handling business at the casino, he found his way to the hole in the wall where she danced. Before I knew it, he told me he was a married man. Emerald had that effect on men, myself included.

Tonight was the grand opening of **EMERALDZ,** and the guest list was already loaded with all the high rollers: musicians, actors, ball players, and drug dealers. Everyone was coming out tonight to see Emerald Vasquez work the pole for old-time's sake. It had been almost seven years since Emerald graced any stage in Vegas, so when news broke that she was opening a gentleman's club and gracing the stage, all of Nevada and beyond went crazy.

"It's looking good in here," I said, walking through the double doors of **EMERALDZ.**

The club had two levels—The lower level was designated for the public, regular folks strolling in after a night of gambling, eager to spend money and gaze at attractive women. The upper level was reserved for VIP guests who could drop 20K and up without blinking. All the private rooms were located upstairs as well. Emerald's girls wouldn't be privately entertaining any low-class, broke-ass men, according to Emerald. Both levels featured a gold stage in the center of the room so everyone could see the show. She bypassed the exaggerated neon lights and kept it simple with luxury chandeliers lining the ceilings. The walls were adorned with a beautiful emerald green that complemented the emerald and gold decor. The vibe was mad classy.

"You know a bitch like me wasn't going to settle for some basic-ass strip joint," Emerald said from the bar.

To my dismay, she was taking inventory. I told her we had staff for that, but she insisted on handling it herself. She had seen too many bartenders in the clubs where she worked drinking more than they should and taking bottles home at the end of the night. Sitting at the bar, I watched Emerald count each bottle and jot down whatever she was documenting. She was focused and pretty as hell doing it. I can't even count the number of times I'd come in here and leave hard as fuck. Looking at her did it for me every time.

"What brings you in?" She asked, putting her notepad down and leaning on the bar. My gaze drifted to the melons on her chest. They were nearly falling out of her black V-neck top. "Eyes up here," she said, clearing her throat.

"My bad sexy. You got them big ole titties laid out on the bar like you ready to serve up some of that titty juice." I licked my lips.

"Why must you always be a perv? Did that even sound sexy to you?"

"You do something to me." I reached out and slid my thumb across her bottom lip.

"Does your woman know you in here?" She asked, standing straight.

I hated when she brought up Akira, but she did it every chance she got. She enjoyed watching the look on my face every time she mentioned her name. It's like she knew I was suffering in that relationship.

"No, and it's none of her business. I might move her out so I can move you on in."

"I like my place just fine and I'm not looking to be anybody's stepmother."

"When you going to invite me over?" I asked, intentionally ignoring her comment. I was still keeping Dario's paternity to myself for the time being.

"Rico, what did you come in here for?" She frowned and walked around the bar over to the main floor. "To harass me?"

"Damn, mean ass. I came to check in. See if you need help or anything from me tonight." I followed behind her.

"Thanks for asking, but everything is set. I'm a bit OCD, which is why I'm here. All I need from you is to show up with some racks." She smiled for the first time since I'd come through her doors.

"Trust me, I'm bringing a duffle bag full of cash."

"Promise?"

"I promise."

13

EMERALD VASQUEZ

Emerald: Will I see you?

Stefan: I wouldn't miss it for the world ;)

My last dance was seven years ago, and when I retired from that stage, I was never supposed to grace it again. Stripper had never been my true calling. I was better than that.

After I killed Taj, Stefan instructed me to keep up my daily routines as if nothing had altered, which meant I had to keep working in the club until I could save enough for my dance studio. The only thing that had changed was my living arrangements because my psycho ex-boyfriend burned down my house and skipped town. At least, that's what the story was. Fortunately for me, Taj had no family and far too many enemies. No one cared to ask where he was when he suddenly stopped coming around, not even the bitch I caught him fucking. I'd see her from time to time, but she'd never make eye contact with me.

Seven years later, I was preparing to take the stage, and my nerves were bad. I had gotten used to being the teacher. I didn't have to go all out in my classes, but tonight was special. The City of Sin was coming out just for me. I locked myself in the studio with all my best pole connoisseurs, whom I'd hired to work at **EMERALDZ**, and perfected every trick I had ever learned. My body was exhausted, but I was determined to show everyone I still had it going on.

"It's been almost a decade since we've seen this Goddess work her magic on stage. Her fine ass always knew how to leave an impression, and tonight she felt it was only right to treat us to a special dance for the grand opening of her establishment **EMERALDZ**."

The men and women in attendance cheered as if Queen Bee were coming to the stage as the DJ continued to speak.

"I'm telling you now, if you broke, step y'all tired asses away from the stage. Only real ballers should be in the building tonight," the DJ yelled on the mic. "It is my absolute honor to introduce the woman of the hour. Don't get too hypnotized by those pretty green eyes, thunder thighs, and the ass to match. Come bounce that shit, EMERALD."

"It's *go* time," I said to myself once the beat dropped to "Partition" by Beyoncé.

My top 2 girls declined down the poles on each side of me and entered the crowd. I stepped onto the stage in a custom-made two-piece bra and thong set. I was dripping in emeralds and gold. The glares and dropped jaws let me know I was *that* bitch. I knew I was *that* bitch. I felt sexy as hell, working my way around the stage slow and seductive, whining my hips, whipping my hair, and grinding my pussy. Grasping the pole, I stroked it seductively as I did a slow swirl. Veering around, I spread my thick thighs and whined as my back slid down.

You can do this.

It was time for the real show. The song switched to "Pour It Up" by Rihanna as I ascended the pole. Stopping halfway, I prayed in my head as I leaned back, and my legs formed a V. I bounced to the beat and slid down a few seconds later, stopping myself before I touched the stage.

Money was flying, and men were howling like fucking dogs. Whipping my right leg around, I climbed back up, this time heading to the top, pausing to twerk my ass as I made my way. Straddling the pole, I did a few 360s and then quickly wrapped my legs around the bar as if I were sitting Indian style. Letting my hands free, I held on for dear life and whipped my hair back and forth. A bitch was dizzy, but I had a few more tricks up my sleeve. When I was finished, the stage was covered in 100-dollar bills, and Rico was sitting front and center, drooling on himself.

Taking the mic from my favorite DJ, I thanked everyone for coming out to show me love.

"Thank you all for coming and packing out my spot. When Dominic retired me from the stage, I knew my big ass wouldn't be back up here dancing for dollars." I paused to laugh. "But it was only right I blessed the house."

"You sho is fine," one of the OGs shouted.

"Thank you, baby." I beamed. "To everyone that showed up, just know this is the only time you'll see me up here, but don't be disappointed. I trained the women of **EMERALDZ**, and they'll only get better. Plus, they're all beautiful as hell, so don't be stingy with those dollars. Drink up, enjoy the show, keep your hands to yourselves, and empty those pockets."

Before I could leave the stage entirely, Rico pulled me off and led me up the stairs into one of my Green VIP rooms.

14

RICO ADAMS

Emerald was a got damn magician up on the pole. The lights followed her and only her— dimming out every nigga in the room. I went from being a spectator in the back to a drooling mess right in front. I had to get her attention before she put her business suit back on and turned back into a boss.

"What the hell, Rico?" she snapped when I let her hand go.

"I see why Dominic wifed you up," I said, closing the door behind her. "You are truly something special. I'm willing to get down on one knee right now."

"Nigga, get up and stop being a creep," she said, folding her arms and poking out her hip.

"I'm just saying," I said, grabbing her hand, "I ain't ever seen no shit like that. You're pure perfection, and I need you."

"Thank you, but you didn't have to haul me up here to tell me that." She glared down at me. "On top of that, I don't think your woman would appreciate you up here proposing and shit."

"You know damn well them niggas wasn't going to give me a chance to speak to you, let alone get some quality time in. And Akira ain't got nothing to do with me and you."

"You're right, but this ain't a quality time kind of night, so stop playing and tell me wassup?"

"I brought that duffle bag you asked for," I said, getting off my knee.

When Emerald went home, I gathered 100k and snuck it up to the VIP room before the night started. When I make promises, I like to keep them. I figured if I cashed out, maybe she'd put out for a nigga. For the past six months, she'd been subtly hitting on me. I've noticed the way she looks at a nigga. Those were the eyes of a woman who'd been wondering what the dick was hitting for but was too afraid to take the dick.

"That's for me?" She asked, eyes wide.

"Every last green bill," I said, retrieving and unzipping the bag.

"And what are you expecting from me?" She slanted her head and narrowed her eyes.

"A bit of your time. Maybe a private dance."

"You just got a full show downstairs, Rico." Emerald rolled her eyes and headed to the door.

I pulled her back before she could open it. "Only a dance, Em. It's not like I'm asking you to fuck me, unless that's what you want." I said, gripping my dick. "To be real, I know that's what you want."

Emerald slapped the hell out of me. "You don't know shit."

"I ain't mean no disrespect," I said, massaging my face. We've teased each other plenty, and she never got offended.

"You drag me up here on the opening night of our club and then treat me like a hoe. Everything about this situation is disrespectful. When I asked you to bring money, it wasn't an invitation for you to fuck me."

"Why you tripping?" I snatched her toward me. "You were willing to throw that pussy at me a few months back. Stop acting like you too good for a nigga when I know I'm who you want."

"Let me go," she yelled.

Before I could react, the door swung open, and I was caught looking aggressive as fuck.

"Rico Adams, you're under arrest for the murder of Dominic Vasquez."

"Hell nah," I said, backing away, "I ain't do shit to that man."

"You have the right to remain silent. Anything you say can and will be used against you in court. You have a right to an attorney. If you cannot afford an attorney, one will be appointed for you."

"The fuck is this Emerald?" I asked, but she remained silent. "Stupid bitch. Did you set me up? I should have listened to Akira. She never trust yo ass."

"You're the stupid one," she smirked at me, then rubbed the arm and wrist I had pulled. She was putting on one hell of a show tonight, both on and off stage. "Please escort this man out of my club before he tries to do something crazy."

"We've got it from here, Mrs. Vasquez."

The nigga who cuffed me winked at Emerald, making my thoughts a reality. The bitch set me up, and now she had my bag of money and club.

As the police dragged me out of the club, all eyes were on me. Clenching my jaw, I held my head down. That bitch could have had them escort me out the back, but she wanted all eyes on me. She wanted all the high rollers to know Rico

Adams was a *criminal*, which I wasn't. Akira knew Emerald was up to some shit, but my dick and money-hungry ass didn't want to listen.

Fuck, I thought as my eyes moved towards a patrol car with a woman inside crying.

"Akira?"

15

EMERALD VASQUEZ

THE AFTERMATH…

I knew revenge was sweet, but watching Stefan handcuff Rico and lead him out of the club was euphoric. Knowing that when he made it to that police car, he would see Akira turned me on. I maintained my composure the entire time I waited for my man to come bursting through those doors, trying my hardest to suppress my laughter, knowing what was to come. I wish I could have seen the look on Akira's face when they came bursting into her home, accusing her of killing my husband. Her heart probably stopped for a second, knowing Dario had nowhere to go.

When I learned Dario was Rico's son, my whole plan formed before my eyes after making love to Detective Stefan Brown. That moment on my living room couch officially made us one, and I did not doubt that he'd help me enact my revenge. We put our brains together and knew if we waited patiently and planted evidence carefully, we could come up with a story about how Akira and Rico planned to kill Dominic to take over his business. A scorned lover and an envious business partner joining forces to take over a billion-dollar empire; pure perfection. It was shit you watched in documentaries.

Truthfully, I had planned to fuck Rico and make him my man. Considering how dehydrated he was, it would have been easy for me. Akira would have been angry, but it wouldn't have stopped her money flow. Plus, my man wasn't too happy about me seducing another man to get revenge, and I didn't want to strain what we were starting to build. I couldn't stand a cheating ass man, and now that he was officially mine, I wouldn't turn into the kind of person I hated.

Something about how Stefan *helped* me the night he came to share news about Akira changed something inside me. The badge he wore kept me from getting entangled with him, yet Stefan had been in my corner since the first day he saw me in the strip club. He was a 22-year-old police officer, working his way up to Detective. He had been in my corner for nearly a decade, but I was too blind to recognize that he'd been the one to love me truly. It was unconditional between us.

When it came to how we would deal with Akira and her unpredictability, life in prison would guarantee her a life of misery and give me peace of mind. I was able to get rid of her forever without having to get my hands dirty *again*.

Furthermore, we found a way to get back what was *mine*.

Since the news of Dario being Rico's son came to light, I was the only family Dominic had left. I was the widow who was taken advantage of and conned into believing my husband left me nothing until I found the *true* will Dominic left behind. The casino, the houses, the cars…everything was *mine,* including Dario. It wasn't his fault his parents were fucking morons who couldn't mind their business or keep their hands to themselves. I considered letting him go into the system since he had no family to go to, but I'm not as evil as his parents make me out to be. They should consider themselves lucky. He has everything he needs and more with me.

"Dinner's almost ready," I yelled to Stefan, who was in the backyard tending to the garden he had planted for me and filled with my favorite flowers.

"I'll be in, in a minute, Pretty Eyes."

"Hurry up. You need to shower before sitting yo ass on my chairs."

"I know better," he yelled back at me, but when my phone rang, I did not hear anything else he said.

"Hello."

"You have a collect call from… *Bitch I'm going to kill you… at* Florence McClure Women's Correctional Center. Press 1 to accept—"

I pressed 1, cutting off the automated voice.

"For someone who wants the world to be convinced they're an innocent woman, you sure don't mind threatening my life over the phone. Don't you know these calls are recorded, stupid?"

"I hate you. I hate you. I hate you," Akira yelled into the phone like a child. "I hope you fucking die. You know I didn't kill him. I loved him!"

"How many times will you call my phone telling these lies? The jury found you and your snake-ass boyfriend guilty. Stop calling my phone before I go back to the judge," I said, putting on my finest accent.

"If I don't kill you, someone will. I promise you," Akira shouted at me through the phone.

"I'll tell our son you said hello." I laughed and hung up.

67

She called back, but I deliberately dismissed her to make her suffer more. You'd think she'd be friendlier to me since her son is under my care, but *nope*. Dario will forget all about her if I want him to. He started calling me Mom a few months ago. It's not as bad as I thought it would be. He just turned seven and is one of the most intelligent kids I've ever been around. We've become closer than I expected. His parents never changed his name, so he's still a Vasquez. Stefan likes my nurturing side, and I've embraced it too. To my surprise, he's fantastic with children. He had me contemplating giving him one.

"Dario."

"Yes, Mommy."

"Get washed up. Dinner's almost ready."

"Was that her again?" Stefan said, kissing me on the cheek.

"Just like clockwork."

"Someone should have told her life ain't easy when Emerald's out for Revenge."

"Let's keep that between me and you, *Detective*."

About the Author

Sydney Reneé is a native of the Bay Area, a mother of one, and a distinguished San Jose State University graduate with a degree in Journalism and Child and Adolescent Development. While attending college, she wrote for the university's newspaper and interned for a magazine, writing lifestyle blogs. Her professional background encompasses both the film and television industry and the realm of Generative AI, in which she helps develop and improve chat/voice bots for telecommunication companies. Sydney discovered her passion for writing at seventeen, a passion that has continuously intensified. Her narratives explore the intricate tapestry of Black womanhood, examining the joys and challenges inherent in love, heartbreak, friendship, career aspirations, and the daily triumphs and tribulations that influence our lives. Sydney Reneé's writing endeavors to inspire women to wholeheartedly embrace their journeys, serving as a reminder that it is never too late to pursue their dreams and to authentically express their true selves.

If you loved her novella, we would be so grateful if you could take a moment to leave a rating or share your thoughts on your favorite platform! To stay connected with all things Sydney Reneé, be sure to follow her author platforms: @theauthorsydneyrenee

Books by Sydney Reneé

Emerald's Revenge Series

Emerald's Revenge: Sin in the City
Emerald's Revenge 2: Escaping my Enemies

Let's Be Friends Series

Let's Be Friends
Let's Be Friends... Again
Let's Be Friends.. Always

Love in Maple Series

Our First Christmas: Skye and Desmond
The Beginning of Our Ending

Stand Alone Books

In Love with an Oakland Hot Boy